What Was Communism?

A SERIES EDITED BY TARIQ ALI

The theory of Communism as enunciated by Marx and En-gels in *The Communist Manifesto* spoke the language of freedom, allied to reason. A freedom from exploitation in conditions that were being created by the dynamic expansion of capital-ism so that 'all that is solid melts into air'. The system was creating its own grave-diggers. But capitalism survived. It was the regimes claiming loyalty to the teachings of Marx that collapsed and reinvented themselves. What went wrong?

This series of books explores the practice of twentieth-century Communism. Was the collapse inevitable? What actually happened in different parts of the world? And is there anything from that experience that can or should be rehabilitated? Why have so many heaven-stormers become submissive and gone over to the camp of reaction? With capitalism mired in a deep crisis, these questions become relevant once again. Marx's philosophy began to be regarded as a finely spun web of abstract and lofty arguments, but one that had failed the test of experience. Perhaps, some argued, it would have been better if his followers had remained idle dreamers and refrained from political activity. The Communist system lasted 70 years and failed only once. Capitalism has existed for over half a millennium and failed regularly. Why is one collapse considered the final and the other episodic? These are some of the questions explored in a variety of ways by writers from all over the globe, many living in countries that once considered themselves Communist states.

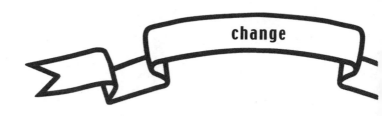

change

MO YAN

TRANSLATED
BY HOWARD GOLDBLATT

Seagull
BOOKS

LONDON NEW YORK CALCUTTA

Seagull Books 2010

Original © Mo Yan 2010
English language translation © Howard Goldblatt 2010

ISBN-13   978 1 9064 9 748 4

British Library Cataloguing-in-Publication Data
A catalogue record for this book is available
from the British Library

Jacket and book designed by Sunandini Banerjee, Seagull Books
Printed at Leelabati Printers, Calcutta, India

1

By rights, I should be narrating events that occurred after 1979, but my thoughts keep carrying me back to that fall afternoon in 1969, when the sun shone brightly, the golden chrysanthemums were in full bloom and the wild geese were on their southern migration. When it reaches that point, I cannot be separated from my thoughts. My memories comprise the 'me' of those days, a lonely boy who had been expelled from school but who was drawn to the clamour inside the schoolyard. I had slipped in through the untended gate, my heart in my throat, and crossed the long, gloomy corridor to enter the school's central quadrangle, a yard surrounded by buildings. To the left stood an oak pole with a cross-bar held on by wire, from which hung a rusty iron bell. Off to the left, two people were playing ping-pong across a simple concrete table on a brick stand, watched eagerly by a crowd that was the source of the clamour. It was the school's fall break and, though most of the spectators were teachers, there were also a few of the pretty co-eds who made up the ping-pong team and who were the pride of the school. They were in training for a countywide tour-nament as part of the October First National Day celebration, so instead of leaving school for the break, they'd stayed behind to practise. As children of the state farm Communist Party cadres, they were well developed and fair-skinned, thanks to a nutri-tious diet. They were also dressed in gaily coloured clothes, and one look told you that they were in a different class from us poor kids. We looked up to them, but they wouldn't give us the time of day.

One of the players was the math teacher, Liu Tianguang, a short man with a startlingly large mouth. We'd heard that he could fit his entire fist in that mouth, but none of us had ever seen him do it. An image of him up at the podium yawning grandly often flashed into my mind—that gaping mouth of his really was a sight to behold. One of his nick-names was 'Hippo'. Now, none of us had ever seen a real hippopotamus, which in Chinese is *hema*, and that sounds like *hama*, for toad, another creature with a large mouth, so it was only natural that we started calling him Toad Liu. That wasn't my invention but, after asking around, he decided it was. Saddling Toad Liu, son of a martyr and deputy chairman of the school's revolutionary committee, with a nick-name was such a heinous offence that expelling me from school and kicking me off campus was both reasonable and inevitable.

I'd always been a diffident kid with lousy luck who was often too clever for his own good. For ex-ample, if I tried to brown-nose one of the teachers, they'd figure I was trying to get them into trouble. I can't count the number of times my mother said to me, 'Son, you're the owl that ruins its reputation by announcing good news!' She was right. No one ever associated me with anything good or worthwhile. But let something bad happen, and all fingers pointed to me. People said I was rebellious, that the quality of my thinking was poor, that I hated school and my teachers. They could not have been more wrong! Truth is, I loved school and had special feelings toward my teacher, Big Mouth Liu. That's because I was a kid who was burdened with a large mouth. The boy in one of my stories—'Large Mouth'—was based on yours truly. Teacher Liu and I were, truth be told, fellow sufferers and ought to have enjoyed mutual understanding or, at the very least, mutual sympathy. If there was one person I'd never have given a nickname to, it was him. Anyone could have seen that. Anyone but him. He dragged me by the hair to his office, he kicked me to the floor and yelled: 'You . . . you . . . you're like a blackbird mocking a black pig! Go take a good look at that dainty mouth of yours in a puddle of your own piss!'

I tried to explain but he wouldn't let me, and that is how a pretty good boy who was fond of Big Mouth Liu—me, Big Mouth Mo—was expelled from school. Despite the fact that Teacher Liu broadcast my shameful expulsion in front of everyone, I still liked my school so much that I looked for ways to sneak into the schoolyard, beat-up book bag slung over my shoulder, every single day.

At first, Teacher Liu personally demanded that I leave. When I refused, he dragged me out by my ear or hair. But I'd sneak right back in before he'd made it back to his office. So then he told some of the bigger boys to do it for him, and, when I still wouldn't leave, they'd pick me up, carry me out beyond the gate and deposit me on the street. But before they were back in their classroom, I was in the schoolyard again, crouching in a corner by the wall, shrunk into myself, both to keep from being spotted and to get a little sympathy as I listened to the cheerful voices and watched the kids jump and play. Ping-pong was my favourite. I could watch that till I lost track of where I was, often with tears in my eyes or biting down on my fist. After a while, they gave up trying to drive me away.

On this particular fall afternoon, forty years ago, I was crouching in the corner, watching Toad Liu brandish a ping-pong paddle of his own design—extra large and shaped like the head of an army shovel—in a match against a girl in my class, Lu Wenli. She too had a large mouth, if you want to know the truth, but hers fit her face perfectly, not oversized like Liu's and mine. Even back then, when a large mouth was not considered a sign of beauty, she was one of the school's best-looking girls. What made her even more appealing was that her father drove the state farm Gaz 51 truck, which to us was lightning fast and eye-popping impressive. In those days, truck drivers were the next thing to royalty.

Once, when I was still in school, the teacher had us write an essay on the topic 'My Ideal', and half the boys in class put down 'truck driver'. But He Zhiwu, a tall, strapping boy with acne and a noticeable moustache—which made him seem more like twenty-five than our age—wrote simply: 'I don't have any other ideal—I only have one ideal—My ideal is to be Lu Wenli's father.'

Teacher Zhang was in the habit of reading the best and worst essays in front of the whole class. But instead of telling us who wrote them, he'd make us guess after he finished. In rural areas back then, the locals laughed at people who spoke Mandarin, even in school. Teacher Zhang was the only one who dared to teach us in that alien dialect. A graduate of a teachers' college, he was still only in his early twenties. He had a gaunt, pale face, wore his hair short with a part down one side and dressed in a faded blue gabardine army jacket, with a pair of paperclips on the collar and blue oversleeves. He must have worn other jackets in different colours and styles, since he couldn't have worn the same one all year round. But that one is inextricably tied to his image in my memory, starting with the oversleeves and paperclips to the jacket itself and then to his face, his features, his voice and his expression. If I don't do that, I simply cannot conjure up his image. In the slang of the 1980s, he would be called 'Butterball', what in the 1990s became 'Pretty Boy'. These days, he'd just be 'Handsome', I guess.

There are probably more fashionable, more popular ways of describing a good-looking young man, but I'll have to check with a neighbour girl to be sure.

He Zhiwu looked considerably older than Teacher Zhang. To say he could have been Zhang's father would be an exaggeration, but no one would dispute the claim that he could have been Zhang's uncle. I still recall how Teacher Zhang stood in front of the class and read He Zhiwu's essay in a hyperbolic, snide tone of voice: 'I don't have any other ideal—I only have one ideal—My ideal is to be Lu Wenli's father—'

Well, after a brief, stunned silence, we almost doubled up laughing. Those three sentences were the sum total of the essay, which the teacher held by a corner and shook hard, as if trying to coax something more out of it.

'Brilliant, truly brilliant!' Teacher Zhang said. 'Now let's see if you can guess which brilliant mind wrote it.' We had no idea, so we looked from side to side and front to back, hoping to spot the author of this 'brilliant' essay, and our gazes fell on the face of He Zhiwu. As the biggest and strongest student in our class, he had a tendency to pick on his deskmate, so Teacher Zhang had put him at the last two-student desk in the back, all by himself. With everyone's eyes on him, his face reddened a bit, it seemed, and we thought he might be embarrassed. But a closer look proved that to be untrue. He actually looked pretty pleased with himself, as we could tell from the foolish, mischievous, almost crafty smirk on his face. Since his upper lip was shorter than the lower one, his upper teeth were exposed when he smiled—purple gums, yellow teeth and a gap in front. One of his favourite tricks was blowing little bubbles through that gap and watching them float seductively in the air. That was what he started doing now, just as the teacher flung the essay book at him like a Frisbee. It only made it as far as the desk occupied by Du Baohua—one of the really good students—

Disgusted, she picked it up and tossed it behind her. 'He Zhiwu,' Teacher Zhang said, 'tell us why you'd like to be Lu Wenli's father.' But he just kept blowing bubbles. 'On your feet!' Zhang demanded. He Zhiwu stood up, looking both haughty and nonchalant. 'Tell us! Why do you want to be Lu Wenli's father?'

Another outburst of laughter caused Lu Wenli, my deskmate, to lay her head down on the desk and burst out crying.

To this day, I don't know why.

He Zhiwu looked haughtier than ever as he ignored the teacher's question, but Lu Wenli's sobbing complicated what had begun as a simple classroom incident, and He's attitude constituted a direct challenge to Zhang's authority as a teacher. In retrospect, if Zhang had known how this was going to turn out, he would not have read He's essay in front of the class— at least that's what I think. But you can't retrieve the arrow after it's left the bow, so he sucked it up and ordered: 'Get out! Roll on out of here!' he said, using a popular cliché.

Without missing a beat, our brilliant classmate, He Zhiwu, picked up his school bag, lay down on the floor, curled up into a ball and started rolling down the space between the two rows of desks. An eruption of laughter died as soon as it left our throats and the mood in the classroom abruptly turned dead serious. All of a sudden, this was no laughing matter; a pall of seriousness had been created by the white-hot anger on the teacher's face and the sound of Lu Wenli's sobs. Meanwhile, He Zhiwu's rolls were not going smoothly—he couldn't control the direction of his movement and kept bumping into desk and bench legs which forced him to adjust his progress. Thanks to all the mud we had tracked in, the brick floor was bumpy and uneven. If it had been me down there, I can imagine how uncomfortable it would have been. But no one was as uncomfortable as Zhang. Our classmate's discomfort was physical; our teacher's was mental. Punishing someone by hurting yourself is nothing to be proud of, and is considered rather thuggish behaviour. But anyone capable of doing it, in my opinion, is no run-of-the-mill thug. There is a heroic side to the behaviour of a thug, and a thuggish side to the behaviour of a hero. So was He Zhiwu a big-time thug or a big-time hero? Don't ask me! But I'll tell you one thing: he is the major character in this narrative, and I'll leave it up to you to decide.

He rolled all the way out of the classroom, stood up and walked off, covered with mud, and without a backward glance. Teacher Zhang yelled out, 'Stop right there!' but He kept walking. It was a bright, sunny day, with a couple of magpies twittering in the branches of a poplar outside the classroom. It almost seemed as if beams of golden light radiated off of He's body, and, although I couldn't say what was going on in everyone else's mind, in my mind, at that moment, he was a decidedly heroic character as he strode ahead, honour-bound not to turn back. Then pieces of shredded paper began falling from his hand and swirling in the air briefly before falling onto the dusty road. I don't know about my classmates, but I was so juiced my heart was pounding. He was actually shredding his textbook! He was ripping up his notebook! He was making a clean break with the school, moving it from the front of his mind all the way to the back, and squashing the teacher under his feet. He was like a bird leaving its cage, free, no longer governed by regulations or school discipline. The rest of us? We had to keep putting up with the teachers' suffocating control. What complicated the issue was that when He Zhiwu rolled out of the classroom, tore up his books and broke with the school, he not only earned my admiration but also had me dreaming of pulling off a similar stunt one day. Not long after this, Big Mouth Liu kicked me out of school and that just about broke my heart. Wrapped up in a deep fondness for school, I was tortured by having to leave it. So who was the hero and who the coward? It should be clear to anyone who reads this.

Lu Wenli was still crying even after He Zhiwu had left. 'That's enough!' Teacher Zhang said with obvious impatience. 'He wasn't saying he really wanted to be your father, he only meant he wanted to be a truck driver *like* your father. Besides, even if he wanted to be your father, would that make him your dad?' Lu Wenli looked up at the teacher, took out a handkerchief and dried her eyes. No more crying. She had big eyes, set far apart, which gave her a sort of foolish expression when she looked at you.

Why did we put Lu Wenli's father on a pedestal? Speed. Boys worship speed. If we heard engine sounds when we were eating, we'd put down our bowls and run to the head of the lane in time to see her father speed by in his Gaz 51. It made no difference where he was headed, he invariably sent terrified chickens scrounging for food in the dusty road flying out of his way and lazy dogs fleeing into roadside ditches. Simply stated, when that truck came along, chickens flew and dogs leaped. Unavoidably, some were run over, but he never slowed down. The chicken's owner or dog's master would quietly pick up the carcass and carry or drag it home. No one ever raised a stink or went looking for him. That truck was all about speed—it's what made it a truck. Chickens and dogs avoid trucks, not the other way around. We were told that the Gaz 51 was a Soviet truck, leftover materiel from the 1950s War to Resist US Aggression and Aid Korea. The bullet holes from US planes in the cab served as proof that it was a truck bathed in glory. When the flames of war blazed, it had charged ahead heroically amid a hail of bullets, and now, during peacetime, it raised a cloud of dust as it tore down the road. When it passed by, we could see the smug look on the face of Wenli's father through the window glass. Some of the time he wore dark sunglasses, at others he didn't; some of the time he had on white gloves, at others he didn't. I preferred it when he wore both gloves and sunglasses. The reason is simple: I'd seen a war movie once, where one of our agents, dressed up as an enemy general with white gloves and dark sunglasses, was on an inspection tour of enemy artillery positions. He reached into the barrel of one of the big guns, and, when he pulled his hand out, the fingers of his glove were smudged. 'Is that any way to take care of military equipment?' he growled in conventional official fashion.

The enemy uniform looked especially smart on one of our fearless agents, the epitome of a heroic spirit. He had real class. For a long while after seeing that movie, we had a great time dressing up and talking like him. 'Is that any way to take care of military equipment?' But the effect was spoiled by the absence of white gloves, hence getting a pair was our fondest dream. The uniform and sunglasses, plus the revolver hanging on his belt, were way beyond our wildest dreams. All the boys and some of the girls in our class worshipped He Zhiwu, not just because of the fascinating way he'd chosen to leave school but also because, shortly after he left, he put on a show with great flair for the whole school, teachers and students.

It was the first of June, Children's Day, and we had all crowded onto the playground for the flag-raising ceremony. Even though our school was out in the sticks, it wasn't too far from the state farm, where there was a group of skilled individuals who had been labelled rightists. Some of them, who had rich experience in sports and recreation, came over as substitute teachers. Thanks to their coaching, Lu Wenli took first place in the Gaomi ping-pong tournament, and Hou Dejun took first place in the junior pole vault at a meet in Changwei. They also helped us form a pretty decent military band. We had a bass drum and ten hip drums, two gongs, ten trumpets, ten trombones, plus two shiny, wraparound tubas, their bells pointing straight up. Now, country folk are no strangers to cymbals and drums: a drumbeat, the clang of a gong and the crash of cymbals: *bong bong clang, bong bong clang, bong clang bong clang bong bong clang*. Boring, monotonous, local noise-making. But the first time we showed off what we could do on the playground—our style, our flair, our appeal, not to mention the high-spirited rhythms and melodies—really opened the villagers' eyes and set their eardrums vibrating. Had any of them ever seen an honour guard? Had they ever heard music quite like that?

The school supplied uniforms for every member of the band: blue shorts and white shirts for the boys, white shirts and blue skirts for the girls, white

rubber-soled shoes and knee-high socks for everyone. Cheeks were rouged, eyebrows were darkened
with charcoal pencils. The girls' braids were tied up
with red ribbons, the boys wore red bow-ties. It was
a thing of beauty, especially since they wore thin
white gloves! All those instruments and uniforms did
not come cheap, easily more than we could have gotten even by selling off the school's desks, chairs,
stools and iron bell. But for the Jiao River State
Farm, it was like a single feather on a hen's body (a
single hair on nine oxen would be an exaggeration).
That farm has appeared in many of my stories and
novels, as have the rightists who always seemed to
me to be pleasure-seekers addicted to carnal pleas-
ures. They are, in fact, the protagonists in my novella
A Long-Distance Race Thirty Years Ago, and I invite anyone who is interested in them to give it a read. But
that is fiction, filled with made-up foolishness, while
this is essentially a memoir, and if not everything I
write is historically accurate that's because after all
these years there are gaps in my memory.

The Jiao River State Farm, which belonged to all the people, had originally been part of the still functioning Xinjiang Production and Construction Corps. For the most part, its members were military retirees; later on, its numbers were increased by the addition of 'educated youths' from Qingdao. In the early 1960s, when our backward village was still using oxcarts and wooden plows, the Jiao River State Farm owned a red Soviet-made combine. When that machine first rumbled onto the farm's vast wheat field, the effect on us was as great as that which our grandparents experienced in 1904, when they saw the first train on the Qingdao–Jinan line, its German locomotive chugging past our village and sending dense black smoke into the air. For a massive enterprise like that, outfitting a primary school military band was too small to be a challenge, like giving the Han dynasty heroic figure Zhang Fei a plate of bean sprouts. (If you are reading this, please forgive me for being long-winded. My head is crammed full of these assorted memories, and I don't mean to write them down—they just flow out of their own accord.)

Why in the world was the Jiao River State Farm willing to outfit a rural, primary-school military band? Simple: many of the students were sons and daughters of influential farm members. And why would they send their rightists as substitute teachers? Same reason. Our local teacher, Zhang, as we've seen, was a graduate of a teachers' college, while Big Mouth Liu never made it past higher primary school. In contrast, the rightists sent over by the farm were educated intellectuals. By this point in my narrative, I'm sure you've figured out that geography made our primary school the finest anywhere on the Shandong Peninsula. I'd been kicked out in the fifth grade, and yet, after I joined the army and was deployed, I was better educated than comrades who had gone to high school elsewhere. If I'd managed to graduate, I might have been admitted to Peking or Qinghua University in 1977, the year the college entrance exams were reinstated.

As we were playing 'The East Is Red' and watching the Five Star flag slowly climb up the flagpole, He Zhiwu appeared in the most conspicuous spot on the playground, wearing a faded, old-style army uniform, a nearly new, wide-brimmed army cap, white gloves and sunglasses· and carrying a homemade horsewhip. Why were we playing 'The East Is Red' during the flag-raising ceremony instead of the National Anthem? Because the men who had written the National Anthem, melody and lyrics, had both been the targets of political campaigns. Where in the world had He Zhiwu gotten his hands on that outfit, we wondered? At the time we had no idea, but years later, when we were together in Qingdao, I asked him. He just laughed and said, half in jest, 'From Lu Wenli's father.' Now, while it would be a stretch to say he'd risen to the level of a fearless spy in a movie, the sight was enough for us to be thunderstruck. Striding purposefully, head high, chest out, he walked down the space between us students and the school leadership, without a hint of fear in his eyes. He pointed his horsewhip at us and, in an affected tone of voice, said, 'Is that any way to take care of military equipment?'

The school administrators stood slack-jawed and wide-eyed as He swaggered past them, then turned and swaggered back before walking into a lane, whistling a tune. We followed him with our eyes as he headed toward the riverbank, up one slope and down the other, and finally disappeared into the river to, we assumed, take off his costume and perhaps have a bath. Or perhaps simply gaze at his reflection. After that, any organized school activity failed to spark interest in us. Nothing, not poetry recitations and not comic performances, could take our minds off of the riverbank. 'We're going to fix his wagon, but good!' a nearly apoplectic Big Mouth Liu sputtered.

But they never did. He Zhiwu's father had been a contract farmhand for decades, and his mother was a veteran Party member, a pockmarked woman with large feet and a mercurial temper that was often displayed when she stood on the millstone in front of their house and cursed a blue streak for no reason that we could fathom. She'd stand there with one hand on her hip, the other up in the air, looking like an old-fashioned teapot. Zhiwu had five younger siblings—three boys and two girls—all of whom shared a tumbledown three-room house that didn't even have straw mats on the brick beds. Not even Chairman Mao would have known how to deal with someone from that background, let alone Big Mouth Liu.

In the fall of 1973, I found temporary work in a cotton processing plant where my uncle was an accountant. Temporary it might have been but, every month, after turning twenty-four yuan over to the production team, I took home fifteen. Back then, with pork selling for seventy cents a catty and eggs at six cents apiece, fifteen yuan went a long way. I began to dress smartly, wore my hair long and owned several pairs of white gloves. All that 'wealth' sort of turned my head. One day, after I got off work, He Zhiwu came to see me. He was wearing worn-out shoes with holes in the toes and a folded blanket over his shoulders. His hair was a mess, he hadn't shaved in a long time and there were three deep creases in his forehead. 'Lend me ten yuan,' he said. 'I'm heading up north.'

'What about your family, what'll they do after you leave?'

'The Communist Party won't let them starve,' he said.

'What'll you do up there?'

'Don't know. But it's better than hanging around here till I die, don't you think? Look at me, I'm damn near thirty and I don't even have a wife. I have to get out of here. Moving kills trees, but it keeps people alive.'

To tell the truth, I didn't want to lend him the ten yuan, a tidy sum in those days.

'How's this?' he said, 'If I make good I won't pay you back, but if I don't I'll pay you back if I have to sell my blood to do it.' I couldn't make heads or tails of his logic, and hemmed and hawed for a while before finally lending him the money.

But let's return to that afternoon when I was leaning against the schoolyard wall, watching a ping-pong match between Big Mouth Liu and Lu Wenli. Liu was a mediocre player who was obsessed with the sport and loved to play against the girls on the team. None of them could be called unattractive, but Lu Wenli was the prettiest and hence his favourite opponent. Every time he hit the ball, he inadvertently opened his gaping mouth. That alone would not have been worth mentioning, but a guttural *gaji gaji* sound emerged, as if a few toads were trying to get out. Sight and sound, his playing style nearly made us gag. Lu Wenli hated playing with Teacher Liu, I knew that, but he was one of the school's administrators so she had no choice. The look on her face and her sloppy play when she was on the other side of the table with Teacher Liu told us all we needed to know about what she was feeling—disgust and loathing.

Now, all this jabbering has been intended to set up the following dramatic scene: with his mouth open, Teacher Liu hit a topspin lob which Lu Wenli casually returned. But as if it had eyes, the glistening ping-pong ball flew right into his mouth.

We were stunned, but only for a moment. Then we burst out laughing. A teacher by the name of Ma, whose face was red to begin with, turned the colour of a rooster's coxcomb. Lu Wenli, who had pulled a long face, chuckled aloud. I was the only one who didn't laugh. I just stood there amazed at what had happened, and recalled a well-known tale from our village that our storyteller Grandpa Wang Gui had told us. Once, when a down-and-outer named Jiang Ziya was selling wheat flour, a strong gale swept it out of his hand. Then he tried selling charcoal, but it was a particularly warm winter. Finally, when he looked up into the sky and sighed, bird shit landed in his mouth. Twenty years later, in the fall of 1999, I was on the subway on my way to work at the *Prosecutorial Daily* when a newspaper peddler caught my attention with: 'Read All About It—Soviet Artillery Shell Lands Right in the Barrel of a German Artillery Piece during the Second World War!' And I immediately thought back to the day when Lu Wenli hit a ping-pong ball into Teacher Liu's mouth. What happened next was that everyone realized they shouldn't be laughing and stopped abruptly. Now, you'd have thought that Liu would have spit the ball out and said something funny—he had a pretty good sense of humour—while Lu Wenli, who was noticeably embarrassed, would have apologized to her teacher. But you'd have been wrong. Instead of spitting it out, Liu stretched out his neck, opened his eyes wide and tried to swallow the thing—we all saw it. Then he flailed his arms as a strange guttural sound emerged from his throat, and he looked like a chicken that's swallowed a poisonous bug. We were flabbergasted and utterly helpless. All but Teacher Zhang, who rushed up and began thumping Liu on the back. Then a teacher named Yu ran up and put his hands around Liu's neck. Arms flailing, Liu pushed them both away. Teacher Wang, one of the rightists and a graduate of a medical college, knew what to do. He ran up, shoved Zhang and Yu out of the way, wrapped his arms—he had long monkey arms—around Liu's waist and jerked his hands into the midsection. The ball flew out of Liu's mouth and landed on the table, where it bounced a time or two and then fell to the ground and stuck, without rolling an inch. Wang let go and, with a strangled cry, Liu crumpled to the ground as if he were made of mud. Lu Wenli threw her paddle down on the table, buried her face in her hands and ran off crying. Wang massaged Teacher Liu, who was lying on the ground, until he was helped up. As soon as he was back on his feet, he looked around and said hoarsely:

'Where's Lu Wenli? Where is she? The little brat damn near killed me!'

2

After I saw He Zhiwu off, I began to fret. Temporary work at the cotton processing plant was better than farming in the village, but I was still listed as a peasant, and if that didn't change, I'd remain stuck on society's bottom rung. At the time, a dozen or so youngsters in the plant had been promoted from temporary to regular workers and were strutting around proudly in leather shoes, with shiny new watches on their wrists. Since I had read classics like *The Three Kingdoms*, *Dream of the Red Chamber* and *Jour-*

ney to the West, had memorized plenty of Tang and Song poems and had pretty good calligraphy for my age, a retired worker at the plant regularly asked me to write letters to his son, a soldier in Hangzhou. I mixed classical and modern prose, using all sorts of ornate phrases that even now make my cheeks and ears burn when I think about them, but the old fellow sang my praises to anyone who would listen, calling me a 'little intellectual'. I actually considered myself pretty special and dreamed of one day displaying my talents to the whole world. I knew that my job at the plant would not last forever and felt that returning to the village would be akin to stabling a racehorse in a cowshed. At the time, admission to college was based not on exams but by recommendations from poor and lower-middle peasants. Even though I met all the requirements for getting into college, realistically, I had two chances—slim and none. Since there weren't even enough slots for the sons and daughters of high-ranking commune cadres, there was no way a fifth-grader like me, an ugly, large-mouthed son of a mid-level peasant, would be picked. So after thinking it over from all angles, joining the army seemed to be the only way of getting out of the village and changing my life.

Getting into the People's Liberation Army was hard, but not as hard as getting into college. So, starting in 1973, I sent in my application and took a physical exam at the commune every year, and every year I was rejected. But then, in February 1976, with the help of some important people, my persistence paid off—I received my enlistment notice. Soon after that, on a cold, snowy day, I walked some fifteen miles to the county town. There I put on an army uniform and climbed into the back of a military truck for the trip to Huang County, where I moved into the famous 'Ding Family Compound' barracks and began basic training.

(I would not revisit the site until the fall of 1999, after Huang County had evolved into the city of Longkou and Ding Family Compound had been converted into a museum. What had originally impressed me as the magnificent home of a wealthy landlord I now saw was little more than a squat building, proof that my horizons had broadened.)

After getting through basic training, I was sent, along with three other recruits, to a so-called Intelligence Unit of the Ministry of Defence. People back home complimented me on my good luck of having been assigned to such a fine unit, but it actually turned out to be a major disappointment—it was only a radio-monitoring station that was about to be phased out.

The command to which we reported was in far off Beijing, so oversight was assigned to the 34th Brigade of the Penglai Garrison Command, stationed in Huang County, and charged with the responsibility of supervising our activities. Supervise! They did their best, but never really could supervise us nor did they dare to. Our unit designation was '263', and any mention of '263' so depressed the commander of the 34th Brigade that his blood pressure would shoot up and his political commissar would simply roll his eyes. That tells you the sort of shitty unit I was assigned to.

When I wasn't tilling the land I was on sentry duty, and the one thing that gave me a good feeling was the unit's truck—just like the one Lu Wenli's father had driven. Same model, same colour, same age. Our driver was a short, grey-haired man with false teeth, a warrant officer in his forties named Zhang. We called him Technician Zhang. His second wife—he was divorced—lived and worked in the city of Jinan with their daughter, while the son he'd had with his first wife lived with him in camp, where they were both basketball fanatics. They were forever shooting hoops, and whoever missed the most shots had to crawl from midcourt to under the basket, pushing the ball along with his head. Soon after I arrived, it was always Technician Zhang who made his son do the crawling. A year later, it was the opposite. The boy, who had a strange name—Qinbing, or Soldier Boy—would whack his father's raised rump with a stick as he crawled on the ground, each whack accompanied by a shout of 'Faster!' His favourite comment was, 'You're like a bean sprout in a privy acting like a long-tailed maggot!'

I had no grand aspirations back then, since there were only a dozen or so men in my unit, which limited the chances to move up. So when I heard one of the veterans say that Technician Zhang was going to teach one of us recruits how to drive a truck, I hoped I'd be the one. Back in the village, I'd had to be content with watching wide-eyed as Lu Wenli's father sped by in his Gaz 51, raising clouds of dust. I once got close to the truck, and it nearly cost me my life. Wenli's father had parked on the street in front of the supply and marketing co-op to buy cigarettes. I leaped at the chance to get a feel of the truck by jumping onto the bumper and grabbing hold of the tailgate. When Wenli's father came out with his cigarettes, he climbed into the cab and sped off, choking me with road dust. So I let go of the tailgate and was thrown to the ground like a dirt clod. I didn't get right up, but when I did I had a swollen nose and bloody lips. I was sort of dazed, not quite sure how it had happened. I later figured it out: inertia.

But now I rode in a Gaz 51 every week, travelling the four or five miles to the farm. My unit had been given forty acres to farm. Nine of us were officers, who took turns on the creaky machine, which left seven guards to work the field. But two of the men, both from the city of Tianjin, were smooth talkers who didn't do a lick of work. Who was left to do the actual work? I and four others.

Technician Zhang sped down the seaside gravel road to the farm, with either his son or one of the officers in the cab with him. We rode in the back, holding on to the sides, caps tucked firmly into our pants pockets, carefree and happy as our hair blew in the wind, and, as I thought back to the time I'd nearly died from wanting to see how fast the truck could go, I couldn't help but congratulate myself on joining the army.

Zhang drove like a madman. Cars and trucks were extremely rare back then, a time when the country could not boast of a single mile of high-speed highway. We were told that the Japanese had built our gravel road when they invaded China, and that it was considered one of the best in the country—a single lane each way, it was barely wide enough for two cars to pass. Cyclists we passed quickly disappeared into the cloud of dust we raised, and we were often treated to a volley of curses from behind us.

The locals had more backbone than the folks back home. No one had ever made trouble for Lu Wenli's father if he ran over a village dog or chicken. But after Technician Zhang ran over a hen one day, the bird's owner, an old woman, came and stood in the camp commander's doorway, banging on the frame with her cane as she gave him hell. I later learned that she was the model for the glorified militia woman in the movie *Mine Warfare*. Both her sons were high-ranking officers in the PLA.

'You call yourself the Eighth Route Army!' she bellowed. 'Not even the Japs acted like this when they came to the village!' Our camp leaders could not nod their agreement fast enough, bending at the waist and offering her ten yuan. 'Ten yuan?' she sputtered, incredulous. 'That hen laid an egg a day, with double yolks, as a matter of fact. That makes 365 eggs a year, all double-yoked. Five of them make one catty, at five-eighty a catty. What does that come to? Figure it out for yourselves.' What could the commander say? He sent her off with twenty yuan, hoping that was the end of it. But no, she'd barely left the barracks when she returned and demanded to see the driver of the truck that had run over her hen. 'I want to see what kind of man,' she said through shrivelled lips, 'drives a run-down old truck like a rabbit trying to outrun a hunter's bullet.' The commander could not deny her request, so he sent me to fetch Technician Zhang. He stood at attention and snapped off a smart-alecky salute.

'Revolutionary old mother,' he said, 'I admit I was wrong!'

'That's a start, but you have to change. From now on, keep it at fifteen miles an hour when you're in the village. If you don't, I'll plant land mines in the road and blow you out of your skin, you bastard!'

Sometime later, I heard that the always-clever Technician Zhang paid a call on the old woman with a box of pastries, and even asked her to be his symbolic foster mother.

In 1979, two months before I was transferred to the city of Baoding in Hebei, Zhang was transferred to a unit in the Jinan Area Command where he was reunited with his wife as a rear echelon assistant, after being separated for years. His son Qinbing became an army recruit, even though he was only fifteen, assigned to a cultural troupe where he studied Shandong rhythmic storytelling under the renowned artist Gao Yuanjun. Word had it that the old woman's eldest son was a senior official in the military district, and that Zhang owed his transfer and promotion to her.

Zhang's many deficiencies as a soldier were obvious to all: he wore his cap at a jaunty angle, would not button his jacket and looked like a typical movie bandit with his breezy way of walking. He was fond of drinking but it took little to get him drunk, at which time he would hum the salty ditty 'Second Sister Misses Her Husband'. One of his favourite pastimes was flirting with the city girls sent down to the countryside, and he took some of the older village girls with him whenever he drove our truck into town. He had an especially close relationship with one of them, a girl we called Sister Hard Luck. When a sow her father raised had a litter of eight piglets he wanted to sell, Zhang loaded them onto the truck, along with the sow, and drove them to the hog market in town. Despite these un-soldierly traits, he took pains to keep his truck in the best shape possible, devoting Saturdays to preventive maintenance and repair. He knew that truck like the back of his hand and could immediately pinpoint the source of any unusual sound. That bullet-riddled Gaz 51 of ours, a veteran of the Korean War, would have been rusting on a junk heap if Technician Zhang hadn't taken such good care of it.

For some reason, Zhang seemed to like me. I was always the one he asked to help him wash or fix up the truck on Saturdays, and my fellow recruits assumed that he was training me to take over for him one day. I figured they were probably right. Thanks to him, I learned a great deal about the workings of the engine, including how a truck could move so fast. He was surprised when I told him about the Gaz 51

Lu Wenli's father had driven back at the Jiao River State Farm. 'I didn't think there could be more than one of these antiques still in use anywhere in the country,' he said. And he didn't stop there. 'One of these days, I'll drive over to that farm and let the two Gaz 51s meet. These are trucks with souls in their eyes, like trees that give birth to spirits. Any bullet-riddled truck in which martyrs' blood has been spilled and can emerge on four wheels ought to be able to do the same.' What would a meeting of two spirit-trucks be like? I wondered.

Zhang said that he was the ninth man to operate this truck. The first had died a hero's death. Sprawled across the steering wheel after being mortally wounded by an enemy bullet or shrapnel that had shattered the windshield, he had somehow managed to drive his truck out of the battle raging around him before he died. One by one, Zhang recounted the name and birthplace of each of his eight predecessors, the way people recall their ancestral lineage. The truck was a 1951 product of the Gorky plant in the Soviet Union, which made it four years older than me. Zhang's narration of the truck's glorious history produced in me a sense of solemn respect for it and that, in turn, brought me back to the truck driven by Lu Wenli's father. The way I saw it, they were like twin sisters separated at birth. 'Why not twin brothers or a boy and a girl,' you ask? I can't say, but that's how I thought of them back then and it stuck. And just think: I'd been assigned to the Penglai Garrison Command in the Jinan Command Area as a new recruit and, purely by chance, been transferred to this small unit attached to General Staff Headquarters, where there was a Gaz 51. There was a greater probability of this happening to me than for Lu Wenli's ping-pong ball flying into Teacher Liu's mouth, maybe, but not by much. After listening to Zhang relate the glorious history of his truck, I realized that my mission was to help bring these long-separated twin sisters together.

In January 1978 our new camp commander ordered Technician Zhang to deliver forty baskets of apples and a hundred bunches of thick green onions to the command we reported to, which was located in the Beijing suburbs, twelve hundred kilometres as the crow flies. He chose me to go along as his helper, and I couldn't have asked for a cushier assignment. We set out late at night, planning to arrive by early evening the following day. But the truck began acting up soon after we passed a town called Weifang. As long as Zhang kept it under thirty, everything was fine. But any faster than that, and loud pops and puffs of smoke were expelled from the tailpipe. Zhang assumed it was a problem with the oil line, but when he crawled under the truck with a flashlight he could find nothing wrong. So we started up again, and the same thing happened. It was that pitch-black hour just before daybreak and freezing cold, with frost and patches of snow on the ground. After laying a tattered coat on the ground, he crawled back under the truck and examined everything he could see. Still nothing. Back in the cab, we sat there glumly smoking cigarettes. 'Strange,' he muttered, 'fucking bizarre! Truck, old friend, what's gotten into you? We've been together for more than a decade, and old Zhang has never done anything to disrupt our friendship.' Hearing him talk to the truck that way nearly had me quaking in my boots, scared of what might happen next. Once again, I thought about the truck Wenli's father drove. We were a good fifty miles from the Jiao River, not all that far by car or truck, and I wondered if the trucks were getting anxious about their meeting. 'Old friend,' Zhang was saying, 'you've got to work with me here, help me deliver this load of apples and onions to Beijing. On our way home, we'll make a side trip to the Jiao River State Farm so you and your sister can meet.' Obviously, Technician Zhang and I were on the same wavelength.

As the red sun rose into the sky, the white road-side came into view—frost or alkali, I couldn't say— when we crept into Shouguang County's main city, looking for a place to get something to eat. Back then, the 'city' looked like a ghost town—a single road down the middle and one roadside diner which didn't open till eight, according to the sign on the glass door. It actually opened at nine, when all they had left were buns from the day before. The waiter

was civil enough—we were, after all, in uniform—
and offered to warm the buns for us. We were also
given a vacuum bottle filled with hot water and a
plate of salted greens. The purchase of a single bun
required a two-ounce grain coupon, but all I had on
me were large-denomination coupons good anywhere in the country. They were too big for the
waiter, who had to go and ask what to do. It was decided that we'd pay thirty cents for every catty's-
worth of grain coupons.

(*In 2003, I was invited to Shouguang to participate in
their vegetable fair. It was now an ultra-modern city with
high-rises, broad avenues and rows of plastic tents that were
altering China's eating patterns, disordering her growing cycles
and changing traditional planting sites. The local residents
were cultivating fruits and vegetables inside those tents that I'd
neither seen nor heard of, and which drew astonished gasps
from traders, both domestic and international.*)

Bellies full, we were back on the road, creeping
along, since our Gaz 51 was still fighting us, sending
loud pops and puffs of smoke out of the tailpipe. It
took longer than it should have, but we eventually

made it to the city of Binzhou, Huimin District, where we went straight to an automotive repair shop and asked an old master mechanic to find out what was wrong. The white-haired old-timer was missing two fingers on his left hand, but that apparently had no effect on the admirable quality of his work. His eyes lit up when he saw us drive in. 'Wow,' he said, 'I'm amazed that this old-timer still runs.' As a friendly gesture, Technician Zhang offered a cigarette to the man, who'd been a mechanic in the Korean War—that made him a comrade of the first driver of our truck, the one who had died sprawled over the steering wheel. With palpable excitement, he walked around the truck and stroked it like a horseman who's reunited with an old steed he'd thought was lost. He climbed into the cab and drove it around the shop's test track a few times. 'It's definitely the oil line,' he said, after he climbed out of the cab and did some checking. But, like Zhang, he could not locate the source of the problem. 'It's old,' he said, finally, 'and you'll just have to make do.' When we asked how much we owed him, he waved us off.

So we were back on the road, spitting and smoking when we tried to speed up. Zhang pulled to the side of the road, laid his head on the steering wheel and didn't move for a long time. 'Technician Zhang,' I said, 'why don't we take the oil line apart and see what we come up with? It's possible that when we took the truck to the garrison repair service before the trip, they put something in the oil line.'

'What could they have put in it? We managed fifty miles an hour from Huang County all the way to Weifang without any trouble.' But he climbed down and watched as I disassembled the oil line all the way up to the oil filter—and then pulled out an earthenware filter cap! 'Well, I'll be damned!' he sputtered. 'What the hell is that?' It turned out that the garrison shop repairman had tried to be helpful by inserting an earthenware filter cap. But its holes were too small and the truck was thus forced to travel at slow speeds only. Zhang threw the thing to the ground and crushed it with the heel of his boot, then grabbed a wrench and put the oil line back together. After wiping his hands with a rag, he put his gloves back on, jumped into the cab, stepped down on the accelerator and off we went at sixty miles an hour. No pops, no smoke, everything back to normal. 'That no-good dick head!' he cursed. 'He damn near choked the life out of this fine steed.' He was excited nearly to the point of giddiness as we sped to Cangzhou like riders on a racehorse, arriving just as the red sun settled below the horizon—too late to go any farther.

When we tried to get a room at the local inn, we were told it was full. But the clerk, a good-hearted, heavy-set young woman, could see how tired we were. 'Comrade soldiers,' she said, 'if you don't mind, I can lay a couple of mats out on the floor.' That sounded all right to us. She then brought us a basin of hot water to wash our feet in, and we were touched by her kindness.

Zhang, who had caught cold from lying on the ground while working on the truck, had developed a bad cough, so I went out to buy some cold medicine. On my way back I took a turn around our truck, which we'd parked by the side of the road, and covered the cab with a tarp. And I patted it on the hood. 'You must be tired,' I said. 'Get some rest.'

We slept like babies that night and got up early the next morning. Zhang's cold was much better. The young woman said we could have a breakfast of oil fritters, flat bread and congee but, if that didn't appeal to us, she'd go out and buy some dumplings if we were willing to wait till eight o'clock. We told her that the inn breakfast sounded fine.

Back on the road. Around noontime, after passing through Tong County, we entered Beijing and drove straight to Chang'an Avenue, where Zhang put the pedal to the metal and shot past every car on the road until we were stopped by a policeman in a blue uniform with white oversleeves and a baton in his hand. He chewed Zhang out for speeding, for which Zhang apologized profusely, saying it was his first time in Beijing and that the traffic laws were new to him. Beijing! My god, this was Beijing! Who'd have believed that on the eighteenth of January 1978, a poor youngster from Northeast Gaomi

Township would find himself in Beijing, sharing a road with black-and-white sedans and green Jeeps? All around me there were high-rises, massive buildings and foreigners with high noses and blue eyes. At the time, the city wasn't one-tenth as big as today's Beijing, but, to my eyes, it was humungous and damned scary.

3

After passing through the city, we continued north along a winding road, through the Juyong Pass, for another hour before we reached the headquarters compound that was our destination. Our load of apples and onions was greeted with considerable excitement, and, once it was unloaded, we were re-loaded with a ping-pong table, four basketballs, ten rifles with practice bayonets, four bayonet shields, twenty practice grenades and two sentry overcoats. On the way over it had just been the two of us, but for the return trip we had company—a new driver for our unit. Tian Hu, a 1977 recruit from Yishui, Shandong, recently graduated from the driver training school, joined us. With big eyes and nice white teeth, he looked young even to me.

We were about to leave Beijing, and who could say if I'd ever make it back—reason enough to feel cheated by only passing through. So we sought permission to spend a few days in the city. Even if it was only one day, at least we could have our picture taken in front of Tiananmen Square—that alone would make the trip worth the trouble. The very accommodating man in charge gave us a three-day pass to see the city and contacted our organization's guesthouse to put us up. Since none of us had a resident's card or a military ID—required by all hotels and guesthouses in the city—we needed a letter of introduction. He gave each of us a letter, with an official red seal, which we could use for lodging along the way.

Our first stop was the Square, where we lined up to have our pictures taken. Then we lined up at the Chairman Mao Mausoleum to pay our respects to the Chairman's remains. As I gazed down at the reposing figure in its crystal sarcophagus, I thought back to the day, two years earlier, when the cataclysmic news of his death had reached us and when I realized that the world had no place for immortals. We'd been convinced that Chairman Mao would never die. We were wrong. We'd also believed that the death of Chairman Mao spelled China's doom. But two years later, she not only continued to exist but also began to thrive. Colleges and universities had opened their doors again; rural landlords and rich peasants had emerged from their demeaned status; peasant families were eating better; and oxen belonging to production teams were fattening up. Why, even someone like me was having his picture taken in front of Tiananmen Square and personally viewing Chairman Mao's remains. Over the next two days, we visited Beihai Park, the Temple of Heaven and, next to it, the Museum of Natural History, where the most impressive exhibit, for us at least, was the dinosaur skeleton. We also took in the sights in the Forbidden City, Jingshan Park, the Summer

Palace, the zoo and bustling Wangfujin. In a shop at Xidan I bought three black leatherette backpacks, one to keep and two for my comrades-in-arms. I also bought a pink scarf for my fiancé, who had been introduced to me by a distant relative when I was working at the cotton processing plant. Seeing that I was a little hesitant, he'd growled, 'Don't be an idiot! When a nice fat pig tries to get in, don't assume it's a dog scratching at your door!'

(*Much later, this distant relative told me he'd wanted to get us together because my uncle was the plant's accountant, and he'd been hoping to use that connection to land a permanent job. After we were married, my wife said, 'Before we met, Standing Committee Member Liu of the commune's Party Committee had tried to make a match for me with the nephew of the commune's Deputy Party Secretary. But I turned it down, complaining that the man had tiny eyes. Then, after you and I were engaged, Liu remarked sarcastically, "You complained that Secretary Guo's nephew had tiny eyes, and now look what you got!" I told him, "Secretary Guo's nephew's eyes are tiny and dull. Mo Yan's eyes are tiny and full of life. There's the difference."' Years later, when I was*

enjoying the undeserved reputation of a writer, Liu remarked
that my wife was a good judge of character.)

The three of us also stood in line for two hours
at a renowned dumpling shop next to Xidan Bazaar,
and treated ourselves to a meal of machine-made
dumplings that were filled with fatty pork that oozed
grease when you bit into them. The machine spat
the things out behind a waist-high counter for customers at the dozen or so tables up front. What a
marvellous invention, I was thinking. The dough,
water and meat went in one end and the finished
dumplings popped out the other, right into a cauldron of boiling water. The product of a mad genius!
When I reported this fantastic news to my mother,
she refused to believe me. Now, when I think back,
the dumplings that machine squeezed out had thick
skins and not much filling, half of which remained
in the cauldron from breaks in the skin. They neither looked nor tasted very good but, at the time, a
meal of machine-made dumplings in a shop next to
Xidan Bazaar gave us boasting rights back home.
Of course, no one eats machine-made dumplings

any more. These days, dumpling shops take pains to advertise that their dumplings are handmade. Fatty pork was the ideal back then; now, vegetarian dumplings are all the rage. That's a decent illustration of how things change.

On the way home, Zhang turned the driving over to Tian Hu and squeezed into the passenger seat with me. The arrival of Tian effectively put an end to my dream of one day becoming a truck driver. When he saw how despondent I was, Zhang gave me a bit of quiet encouragement: 'You're too talented to waste your life as a truck driver. That would be like shooting down a mosquito with a cannon. Be patient. Good fortune will find you one day.' That helped, but who could think of the future at a time like that? How could I accept the fact that I might return home after two years of struggling to make something of myself with nothing to show for it? No, that wasn't for me! I had to keep struggling! I was going to keep fighting!

In Beijing, I dreamed about going back to my village with Technician Zhang and parking our truck and the one driven by Lu Wenli's father in front of my school playground: two Gaz 51s sit side by side, with red silk streamers on the hood and a red silk flower affixed to each hood ornament. The military band is playing for students who are performing a simple rhythmic silk-streamer dance. When night falls and all is quiet, I come alone to the playground under a bright moon and there, like a pair of puppies, the trucks are touching noses to make one another's acquaintance. They bray like a pair of long-separated donkeys. Then they back up a hundred metres or so and drive forward to touch noses for a second, then a third time. With a backward kick, Lu Wenli's father's truck speeds off, followed closely by ours. Two Gaz 51s circle the playground, like a male donkey in pursuit of a female. Then it dawned on me: they weren't twins, they were lovers! The chase was on, followed by mating and the birth of a baby Gaz 51. When I described my dream to my companions, Zhang said, 'It looks like we'll have to pay a visit to the Jiao River State Farm.'

'My father had a dream like that once,' Tian said, 'but he had an accident the next day.' Tian's father was also a truck driver.

'Don't talk like a bad-luck raven, you dumb greenhorn!' Zhang said.

Inauspicious comments like that were taboos to Zhang, and what should have been something to look forward to was spoiled. We reached Weifang around nine o'clock, with stars twinkling in the night sky. 'Little Mo,' Zhang said, 'we've been away a long time. My eyelids have started twitching, and I'm scared that something bad is going to happen to my son, Qinbing. Why don't I take you to the Weifang Train Station, so you can make a trip home? I'll get your leave approved back at camp. If there's a problem, I'll take care of it. Little Tian and I will take the Yan-Wei Highway back to camp.'

I knew how he felt. I'd pictured us entering my village in our Gaz 51 to a spectacular reception many, many times. Now that bubble had burst, and I felt terrible. But a chance to go home for the first time in the two years since I joined the army did not come easily. So Zhang and Tian drove away after dropping me off at the Weifang Train Station. I followed the truck's taillights with my eyes as long as I could, and then went in to buy a ticket.

For the second time in my life I was on a train. The first had been when I had accompanied my older brother and a nephew to Qingdao, where they boarded a ship to Shanghai. It was springtime, and I was eighteen. A train ride was a big deal back then, something I was able to brag about long after my return trip home. I was nearly as excited this time. The train was jam-packed and saturated with the rank smell of urine. A couple of young men got into a fight over a spot in the toilet. One wound up with a bloody nose, the other a torn ear. All this seemed perfectly normal to me at the time. The distance from Weifang to Gaomi was slightly over a hundred kilometres, but the trip took more than three bumpy hours. In 2008, a trip from Beijing to Gaomi, about eight hundred kilometres, on the Harmony Line took only about five hours.

It was early morning when we pulled in to Gaomi Station. The sun had just risen, painting the sky red. I walked out after having my ticket checked, and was immediately struck by *Maoqiang* singing from the traditional opera *Luoshan ji* that emerged from a nearby fritter-and-soymilk shop. The famous slow, desolate, shimmering aria sung by an old woman made me tear up. (*I mentioned this incident a few days ago, during my introduction to* Maoqiang *opera for the Central TV drama channel*.) I went in and bought half a catty of oil fritters and a bowl of soymilk, sat down and listened as I ate.

Both sides of the square in front of the station were lined with peddlers trying to attract customers for whatever they were selling. Two years before that, the only place where you could get something to eat near the station had been the state-run restaurant with its abominable service. Then small-time entrepreneurs began moving in, and, within a few years, private stalls had shot up like bamboo after a spring shower. They were everywhere, while nationalized

and collective restaurants, supply and marketing co-
ops and state-run shops were shutting down.

I boarded a bus for Northeast Township and
didn't arrive at home until three that afternoon. The
sight of that tumbledown house and, even worse,
parents who had grown old since I last saw them was
almost more than I could bear. I told them all about
the situation in camp, how the road to officialdom
was closed to me and my dream to learn to be a
truck driver shattered, and that the best I could man-
age was to come back home after finishing my two-
year stint in the army. 'We thought this was your
chance to make a life for yourself . . .'

'My bad luck,' I said, 'to get that assignment.
If I'd been sent to a field army, I might be an officer
by now.'

'What good does any of this talk do?' my father
said. 'You can see how things are here. Now go back
and do the best you can. Don't be afraid to put yourself out. People die from sickness, not hard work.
Keep at it, and sooner or later your superiors will
take note. If you can't get promoted and they won't

let you learn to drive, then find a way to join the Party. I've been a loyal Communist all my life, but have never been granted entry into the Party. I've got no future, but you have. Find a way to join the Party while you're still in the army. Then you can come home with a bit of dignity.'

4

My commanding officer summoned me soon after I arrived back in camp. He told me we'd been given a slot at the entrance exam for the PLA Engineering and Technical College in Zhengzhou and, after careful deliberation, I'd been chosen to study for the exam. A little explosion went off in my head and my brain stopped functioning for a moment. I recall that we were treated to meatballs at lunch that day, a rare, special treat at the time, but it was the first time I'd eaten meat without tasting it, like chewing wax.

Why was that? Because I was worried. My superiors had chosen me to take the exam on the assumption that I was a high-school graduate, while in fact I hadn't even made it through the fifth grade. I didn't think I'd have any trouble on the language and politics sections, but I was virtually illiterate where math, physics and chemistry were concerned. The open slot specialization was computer terminal repair, a field way beyond my abilities. But revealing my background would have put me out of the running for any opportunity for advancement. So I braced myself and said I'd do my best. A radio technician in camp named Ma, a fellow my age from Hunan said that, as far as he knew, we'd been given the slot out of consideration for being an outstation and that the exam was window dressing—that I'd get in to the college as long as I didn't hand in a blank exam paper. 'But I can't even handle the four basics in arithmetic,' I said, 'and fractions are totally alien to me.'

He offered to coach me. 'There's nothing someone as brainy as you can't master', he said. 'And you've got six months to prepare.' That was all the encouragement I needed to buckle down and give it a shot. The first thing I did was write home and ask them to send my elder brother's middle- and high-school textbooks. Then Technician Ma's quarters became my classroom every night of the week. The camp leadership authorized the use of a desk and chair in the storeroom, so I could study there while not on sentry duty. And in order for me to concentrate on my studies, a 1977 recruit temporarily assumed my duties as deputy unit commander.

My brother had been the first person from Northeast Gaomi Township ever to go to college. That had brought the family so much distinction that following him into college had been a dream of mine since childhood. And now the opportunity to see that dream come true had arrived. But mastering high-school math, physics and chemistry on my own in six months was a formidable challenge. There was no time for practice exercises—all I could do was read and try to understand everything in the textbooks I was sent. I had to memorize all those formulae without worrying if I understood them or not. So I covered the storeroom walls with pencilled formulae as I struggled along, vacillating between hope and despair, mostly the latter. My hopes were dwindling. I grew pale, I lost weight, my hair was a mess—our political instructor said I was beginning to look like a convict. Then, one day in August, he summoned me: 'I just got a phone call,' he said, 'and was told that the exam slot we'd been promised has been rescinded. I expect you to deal with this set-back with the proper attitude.' On the one hand, I felt as if I'd been relieved of a heavy burden, but, on the other, the news came as a major disappointment. The political instructor announced the change to the camp's full complement that day, adding that he was restoring my duties as deputy commander of the se-curity guard.

The announcement came during the high tide of an army-wide literacy campaign, and I was as-signed the job of math instructor for the camp. So I began, and, as I was teaching math to the soldiers, I realized how much I'd learned in a short six months.

One of the officers even came to my lecture on trigonometry and was dutifully impressed. That class was instrumental in my subsequent transfer to the Baoding Training Battalion. My dream of attending college had been shattered, but that only intensified my desire to become a writer. In those days, you could gain national recognition from the publication of a single short story. So I subscribed to two magazines—*People's Literature* and *PLA Arts and Letters*—and, in September 1978, began my study of literary creation. My first effort was a short story I called 'Mama'. I followed that with a six-act play entitled *Divorce*.

A middle-aged man named Sun, who had a deformed left eye, delivered the unit's mail. Everyone called him Old Sun. Everyone, that is, but a few flippant staff officers to whom he was known as 'One-eyed Dragon'. My heart raced every time I heard the sound of his motorbike, hoping for good news regarding the two manuscripts. But the best news I got was a pencilled rejection letter from *PLA Arts and Letters*—*Divorce* was too long for its pages, and I should send it elsewhere. On the eve of my transfer to Baoding, in order to lighten my load and in an effort to start over, I burned both manuscripts. When I returned to the camp in 1999, the barracks were being used to raise chickens. When I went to take a look at the storeroom, I could still make out the math, physics and chemistry formulae I'd written on the walls.

5

Nineteen seventy-nine was a banner year for the
country and for me. On the seventeenth of February,
our military launched a counterattack against Viet-
namese aggression. Two hundred thousand troops
from Guangxi and Yunnan crossed the border into
Vietnam. The next day, while we were at breakfast,
we heard a radio report that a heroic soldier named
Li Chengwen had been killed in the course of blowing up an enemy fortified position. Many of the men
who had enlisted with us had been sent to the front

lines and, deep down, I envied them—I longed for a chance to go to the front and become a hero myself. If I made it back alive, I'd be promoted for my valour; if not, my parents would earn the distinction of a martyr's family, which would dramatically alter their political status. They would not have raised me in vain. And I wasn't the only one who thought that way. It may have been a simple, immature way of thinking, but it was the twisted mindset we children of oppressed middle peasants had developed. A glorious death was better than a demeaned existence. With fighting at the front, we stopped being an undisciplined unit. We threw ourselves into everything we were expected to do: drills, training, sentry duty or labour. But the war ended quickly, and we immediately reverted to our old ways.

In late June, I received permission to return home to get married. The ceremony took place on the third of July, a rainy day. During my leave, several men who had fought in the war returned home covered in glory and two had even received battlefield promotions. Oh, how I envied them. But what awaited me? Maybe in a few months, I'd leave the army and return home.

The day after the wedding, I rode my bicycle over to the Jiao River State Farm, telling my wife I was going to see some former schoolmates—the real reason was to see the Gaz 51 that Lu Wenli's father had driven, the one that had nearly killed me. I found it in the vehicle lot. Wenli's father was painting it. I walked up, took out a pack of cigarettes and offered him one. 'Master Lu,' I said, 'know who I am?' He shook his head. 'I was Lu Wenli's classmate in primary school. My name is Mo Xie [Yan].'

'Ah, now I know. You're the one who stole a pair of gloves out of my truck that time I parked it at the entrance to your village.'

'That wasn't me,' I said, 'it was He Zhiwu, and he didn't just steal a pair of gloves—he also let the air out of your tyres.'

'Oh, that little prick! We call people like that "crooked-necked geese". He was full of bad ideas. He didn't stop at letting the air out of my tyres—he even took the valve caps with him! After that, he came to borrow my uniform and cap! If I didn't lend them to him, he said he'd throw nails all over the road to puncture my tyres.' That jogged my memory: the truck stalled on the street, one day, with four flat tyres out of six and Lu Wenli's father fuming and cursing. I'd been the prime suspect, as far as the school was concerned, and they questioned me at length. Big Mouth Liu even stuck a hot poker in front of my face and demanded that I confess. But I had nothing to worry about since I hadn't done it, and the poker didn't bother me.

I asked him what Wenli was doing. He said she was working in the county rubber plant. 'Getting a job at the state farm is great,' I said, 'since all the people own it, and the rubber plant is a collective.'

'I thought you knew,' he said. 'The county runs the farm now and the land will be contracted out. Pretty soon there won't be any difference between us and the peasants.'

I pointed to the half-painted truck and to the rusting machines in the vehicle lot. 'What about all these things?'

'We'll sell what we can and let the rest rust away.'

'Are you going to sell the Gaz 51?'

'A few days ago, He Zhiwu sent a telegram from Inner Mongolia saying he'd give me eight thousand yuan for it. That's a lot of money for a beat-up truck. I think the little prick's lost his marbles. Five thousand more and he could buy a Liberation truck fresh off the assembly line. Do you think he's trying to make a fool out of me?'

With a flood of emotions, I thought to myself, 'He Zhiwu, what's that brilliant mind of yours cooking up this time? You've obviously made a pot of money, but why throw so much of it away on a toothless old truck? Is a bit of nostalgia worth it?' 'Master Lu,' I said aloud, 'I don't know what he has in mind, but I doubt that he's trying to make a fool out of you.'

'Well, he can do what he wants', Lu said, 'but I'm not sure I want to sell it. Do you know how many years this truck and I have been together? We've formed a lasting bond.' He went back to his painting. 'Where are you stationed?' he asked after a moment.

'Huang County.'

'That must be the 34th Regiment at the Penglai Garrison Command.'

'We're attached to the General Staff under the supervision of the 34th Regiment.'

'Regiment Commander Xu and I are old comrades-in-arms,' he said. 'He was the regimental training officer when I was a company commander.'

'I heard a report by Commander Xu once,' I said excitedly. 'What a coincidence! Want me to take something back to him? I'm heading back tomorrow.'

'He's a powerful regimental commander,' he said wistfully, 'and I'm just a truck driver. That would look like I was sucking up to him.'

I felt like responding to that, but he'd already gone back to painting the truck. I knew what had happened to him. After returning from the Korean battlefield, he'd been promoted to captain, made a company commander. His future was bright. But like so many young men on the way up, he became arrogant, couldn't keep his pants zipped, and thus ruined what could have been a fine military career.

Early the next day, I went into town to buy a bus ticket back to Huang County. Since I had two hours to kill before the bus left, I decided to make a side trip to the rubber plant, a mere thirty-minute walk. When I told the old gate guard that I was looking for Lu Wenli, he said he thought she was on the night shift. Then he asked me why I wanted to see her. I told him she had been my classmate and since I was passing through the area, I thought I'd look her up and say hello. Noting that I was a soldier, he offered to go see if she was around. 'Thank you,' I said.

'Watch the gate for me while I go find her.' I looked at my wristwatch—I'd borrowed a thirty-yuan Zhongshan watch from one of my buddies—wanting to make sure I didn't miss my bus. What seemed a long time later, I spotted the old guard with Lu Wenli in tow. She'd thrown a coat over her shoulders and was wearing sweatpants as she shuffled along in her slippers. Her hair was uncombed and she had sleep in her eyes. She was yawning.

I walked up and called her by name. After looking me up and down, she said coldly, 'So, it's you. What do you want?'

'Nothing, really,' I said, suddenly feeling awkward, 'I was heading back to my unit . . . had some time before my bus left . . . thought I'd say hello to an old classmate . . . went to the Jiao River State Farm yesterday and saw your father. He told me you were working here . . .'

'If that's all it is,' she said curtly, 'I'm going back to bed.' She turned and walked away. I could not have felt worse as I stared at her back.

I'd only been back in my unit two months when I received transfer orders to the Baoding Training Regiment. The buddy who'd lent me his Zhongshan wristwatch when I went back to get married—we were from the same village—said with a sigh, 'Apparently, marriage brings good luck. I'm going home to do the same in a few days.' Not long before I left

the unit, someone organized a basketball game between the security officers and us. I didn't miss a shot
that day, the best game of my life.

On September 10, I left Huang County with
Technician Ma, who had business in Beijing. Tian
Hu drove us to the Weifang Train Station in the
truck. See you later, Gaz 51. (*No, there'd be no later—
this was a final good-bye. I never did see it again, and I've
often wondered which junkyard it wound up in. As for the one
driven by Lu Wenli's father, people told me that He Zhiwu
did in fact buy it. Before driving it away, he made a couple of
circuits around the school playground, thereby carrying out his
declared ideal of becoming 'Lu Wenli's father'. Then he drove
off in a cloud of dust.*)

At Baoding, I was a squad leader responsible
for training students recruited from that year's high
school class. They would study for two years, the
equivalent of a junior-college programme, and graduate as commissioned officers at Grade 23. Their
speciality was known by a long title, but it boiled
down to putting on a pair of headphones and tran-
scribing telegraphic messages.

When the assignment ended, a month later, I was kept on at the regiment: first, in a security position, then as a political instructor charged with teaching philosophy and political economics—two areas in which I had next to no knowledge. Like a duck that has to be pushed to climb a rack, I forced myself. At first it was exhausting, but I got into the groove after a semester. What happened then was that my down-but-not-out literary aspirations got up off the canvas. In September 1981, after a string of rejections, my first published story, 'A Rainy Spring Night', appeared in the Baoding magazine *Lily Pond*. A second story, 'The Ugly Soldier', appeared in the same magazine the following spring. Now, a common soldier who assumes the duties of an officer, who can eloquently and endlessly reveal the principles of Marxism to a group of students and who can write fiction will inevitably attract attention.

(My daughter was born on the third of November, 1981. When it came to name her, my eldest brother, who was working in Hunan, suggested Ailian [or, a fondness for lilies] be-

cause my first published story appeared in Lily Pond *and after the famous poem by the Song poet Zhou Dunyi* ['Of a Fondness for Lilies']. *That struck me as too common, so I named her Xiaoxiao after a small bamboo flute. But when she started school, her teacher thought there were too many strokes in her name and changed it to Xiaoxiao,* 'to smile', *and it stuck.*)

With the help of a good many military heavy-hitters, in the summer of 1982, when I was back home on leave, I received word that they'd gone outside the rules to promote me as an officer. The order naming me a commissioned training officer is probably still in my dossier. I recall that it was my father who brought the letter home. When I told him what it said, the light in his eyes gave me a warm feeling that had a somewhat bleak edge. Without a word, he picked up his hoe and went out into the fields. His reaction got me thinking about how an elderly distant relative from a neighbouring village had reacted to the news that his son had been promoted: he'd walked around the village beating a gong and shouting, 'My son is an officer! My son is an officer!' My father's low-key dealing with the same issue taught me a lot about his personality, his character, his life experiences.

In 1984, I tested into the Literature Department of the PLA Institute of Art. Shortly thereafter, my story 'The Transparent Carrot' was published to wide acclaim and followed soon by the novella *Red Sorghum*, which made a big splash. During summer break in 1986, when I was shopping in the city market, I ran into a fellow from a neighbouring village who grabbed my arm and shouted, wide-eyed, 'I hear you struck it rich! They say you sold a novel for a million!' A million-yuan novel is always a possibility, of course, but not back then. Yet before I could set him straight, he said, 'Don't worry, I'm not looking for a handout. My son passed an exam to study in America! In a few years, the greenbacks will be rolling in!'

In the fall of 1987, Zhang Yimou brought Gong Li, Jiang Wen and others to Gaomi to film *Red Sorghum*, whose original title had been *Nine-nine at Qingshakou*, after a bloody incident that occurred on the ninth day of the ninth month at a place the locals called 'Qingshakou'. One of the film company minibuses was even spray-painted in red with the words 'Nine-nine at Qingshakou'. So why weren't they going to call it *Red Sorghum* from the beginning, since that's what they wound up with? I didn't ask, and they didn't volunteer an answer. At the time, moviemaking was a novelty to people in Northeast Gaomi Township. Not once since Pangu split Heaven and Earth had anyone ventured out to this remote spot to make a movie. Before they started filming, I invited the cast to dinner. Zhang Yimou and Jiang Wen showed up with shaved heads and deeply tanned bare arms. Gong Li was dressed simply and wore her hair in a rustic fashion. Without makeup, she looked like a girl you might see anywhere. For villagers, who assumed that any woman who acted in movies had to be out-of-this-world gorgeous, Gong Li was a disappointment. Who could have predicted that a decade later she would be an international star, gliding through life with the grace of nobility and flirtatious looks, always the coquette?

They drew an enormous crowd on the day they started filming, including ordinary people who had ridden their bicycles from outlying counties and officials who came in their government cars. They arrived in high spirits and left disappointed.

The cast was put up in the county guesthouse, whose rooms were equipped neither with air conditioning nor private baths, typical of county-level guesthouses throughout the country. Actors back then were not as big a deal as they are now, and, after the cast left, a local friend of mine said, 'People around here have a pretty low opinion of actors, especially that Jiang Wen, who made a long-distance phone call that lasted four hours.'

'Did he pay for it?'

'Yes.'

'So what's the big deal?' I doubt that anyone would get exercised over something like that these days. Moving from 'everyone is involved in everyone else's business' to the protection of individual privacy has been a significant step forward for the Chinese.

Not long ago, I saw an actor from the early 1980s, sentenced to ten years in prison for immorality, plead his case on television and complain that his sentence was unfair. He admitted having consensual sexual relations with several women, which, at the time, was viewed as a serious crime—it was national headline news. Most people were convinced that he got what he deserved. No one felt that the punishment did not fit the crime. If we used the same standards to judge relations between the sexes these days . . . how many more jails would we need to lock the miscreants up?

As soon as I saw the film crew's beat-up vehicle, it reminded me of the Gaz 51 that Lu Wenli's father had driven and subsequently bought by He Zhiwu. They were about the same colour, although on closer inspection the hood was a little different. Villagers knew that He Zhiwu was in Inner Mongolia, and I wondered if his Gaz 51 was still serving him.

6

In August 1988, I was admitted to a graduate programme run jointly by Beijing Normal University
and the Lu Xun Literature Institute. Unlike in 1984,
when I was admitted to the PLA Arts Institute, this
wasn't such a big deal, at least not to me. I'd been almost giddy when the notification for the Arts Institute came, since it fulfilled both of my dreams—to
go to college and to become a writer. This time, as a
graduate student, I'd earn an MA degree. But I was

already pretty well known, I'd figured out what literature was all about and I knew that, for a writer, the writing itself was what mattered, not educational background or college degree. I'd decided not to attend when a friend advised me to take the long view and use it as an opportunity to study English, which would come in handy one day. He was right, of course. So I studied hard for a couple of months and committed a few hundred words to memory. But then the student movement erupted, with tensions mounting daily, and few of us felt like going to class. Having never been long on willpower, I used this as an excuse to put my study on English on hold. As time went on, and I received invitations to visit foreign countries, I had plenty of reason to regret not learning some English when I had the chance. A few years ago, I thought about trying to acquire some basic conversational skills in English—but I've abandoned even that thought. All I can do is hope against hope that some genius will invent a simple, convenient, quick and accurate interpreting gadget. That would make my overseas trips easier.

In the spring of 1990, I returned to the county town where I demolished run-down buildings and, within the space of a month, had four new houses built. While I was doing that, the school sent several telegrams urging me to return. But when I did, the authorities encouraged me to drop out. I didn't even have to think about it—I agreed on the spot. Later on, some classmates spoke up on my behalf and managed to secure the support of Professor Tong of Beijing Normal to keep me in the class. The graduation ceremony took place on the first day of the Gulf War. It was a hurried ceremony, with no party afterward. One of the film department's students gave me a ride home on his three-wheeled motorbike. Since there was no dormitory available, I had to bed down in a scrap warehouse where hordes of rats kept me awake every night. One of them made a nest in my trunk and had a litter of babies. For years afterward, my clothes and bedding smelled of rat urine. I arranged several statues of Chairman Mao that were stored there in the doorway and by my bed to serve as sentries of a sort. Some of my writer friends came to see me, after making their way past the gate guards. When they saw what I'd done, they labelled me China's number one creative genius for making Chairman Mao my sentry and bodyguard. That was my home for two years, until the unit allotted me a two-room apartment. But, even after I moved out, I was nostalgic for the days I'd spent with Chairman Mao.

Someone knocked at my door in the spring of 1992. It was He Zhiwu, after all those years. He smiled when I asked him how he'd managed to find me. 'You don't go to the temple without a reason,' he said after a moment.

'What do you want?' I asked. 'If you need something, I'll do what I can.'

He told me he had a full-time job in a government transportation office in Inner Mongolia, and was looking for a way to get back to Gaomi to take care of his ageing parents. So I wrote a letter to the head of Gaomi County and told He to take it to the county office. When I asked him what happened to the Gaz 51, he stared at me. 'I thought you knew,' he said. 'I sold it to Zhang Yimou's film crew. It was the truck that Jiang Wen and the others loaded with crocks of sorghum liquor and turned into a bomb on wheels.'

So that *was* Lu Wenli's father's Gaz 51!

'So you see, I made a contribution to your movie.'

'But the hood looked different,' I exclaimed.

'You don't get it, do you? That crew was too smart to try to pass off a Soviet truck for a Japanese one without changing it. It wouldn't work—people would spot the difference.'

'How much did you get for it?'

'I sold it as scrap metal. It had sat in my father's yard for years, and I didn't know what to do with it. So when the opportunity to get rid of it came, I gave it a grand send-off.'

I returned to Gaomi over lunar New Year's in early 1993. He Zhiwu came by to tell me he'd been transferred back and was working in the Qingdao Gaomi affairs office. 'You sure know how to get things done,' I said.

'It was your letter that did it.'

Over the years that followed, he often came to Beijing and treated me to expensive meals. Apparently, he was doing quite well. He never failed to invite me to come to Qingdao—he had no more dealings with Gaomi—where he'd opened a flourishing business. 'Any time you come to Qingdao,' he said, 'I'm good for all your expenses.'

He filled me in on what our classmates were doing. He even knew what the teachers were up to. From him I learned that Zhang, our writing teacher, had retired from a position as political instructor at a county high school, and that one of his sons ran a lumber business and the other was Party Secretary of the Chengnan Township Communist Youth League. Big Mouth Liu got as high as Deputy Head of the County Department of Education. After his wife died, he married Lu Wenli, who, despite her youth, had become a widow. Her first husband, the son of a county big shot, was a no-account creep who drank and gambled and whored around. There was even talk that he beat her. Then, one day, he rode his motorbike into a tree. What I wanted to know was how she'd hooked up with Big Mouth Liu. 'That's unbelievable!' I said.

He Zhiwu laughed. 'Is hitting a ping-pong ball into an opponent's mouth believable?'

No, that truly was unbelievable, and it goes to show that the affairs of the world are always in flux, that a happy fate can bring lovers together, that accidents happen all the time, and that the strange and curious are always with us. So what can I say?

7

I made a special trip to Qingdao to see He Zhiwu in August 2008. I'd been to the city before that, either to give lectures or attend meetings, but had always been too rushed to call on him and that did not please him. 'How about coming for three days to talk, just you and me? There's a lot I'd like to tell you, things that will stir your imagination and help you write one hell of a novel. A long time ago you lent me ten yuan, and now I'm going to repay you with material for a novel.'

He reserved a luxury suite in the Huiquan Imperial Hotel with a panoramic view of the ocean, close enough to hear the sound of the waves. I'd no sooner settled in than he began relating his experiences over the past thirty years. For the next three days his mouth never took a break, whether we were sitting around drinking or strolling on the beach. He ordered every imaginable delicacy, nearly all of which I ate alone. 'Help me out here,' I said, 'I can't eat all this, and I'd hate to let it go to waste.'

'You eat,' he said. 'I've got the three "highs": cholesterol, blood pressure and blood sugar, and I can't eat that stuff.' So he just drank and smoked and talked. After telling his driver to take the three days off, he drove us all up and down the coast.

'Should you be doing this, after all you've drunk?'

'Don't worry,' he said, 'I'm like Wu Song—liquor only makes me better at things.'

'But the police don't know that,' I said.

He laughed. 'I don't think they're interested in arresting me.' Being behind the wheel had no effect on his nonstop talking, which was regularly accompanied by hand gestures.

'Don't you think you ought to concentrate on your driving?'

'Don't sweat it. After thirty years of driving, the minute I sit behind the wheel I become one with my vehicle. But Lu Tiangong—now he was a driver. That stone bridge behind the village was barely wide enough to accommodate his Gaz 51, but the guy crossed it without taking his foot off the gas.'

It took me a moment to figure out who Lu Tiangong was, and I realized there was quite a gap between He Zhiwu and me.

'I spent one-twenty of the ten yuan you lent me for a ticket to Weifang, on a local from Qingdao to Shenyang. I wanted to take it all the way to the end, though the ticket only allowed me to go as far as Weifang. The ticket inspection was very tight: a pair of railway cops accompanied the conductor to make sure no one tried to get a free ride. If they caught you, being put off the train was inevitable, sometimes also a beating. A PLA soldier wearing a black mourning band was sitting across from me, and I assumed that one of his parents had died. You know, I studied physiognomy under Grandpa Wang Gui'—as a matter of fact, I didn't know—'so I chatted up my new acquaintance, wanting to get in his good graces. When I told him that his father and I went way back, he believed every word. So I said, "Brother, I've got a problem, one I hope you can help me out with." Well, he reached into his pocket and took out a ticket to Shenyang. "Go on," he said softly, "use this. Then slip it under my teacup when you're finished with it." Just then a server was coming down the aisle with a teapot, so the soldier took it from him and poured tea for the passengers around us. Everyone called him a living Lei Feng. PLA soldiers were at the top of the pecking order back then. With his help, I made it to Shenyang with no trouble. My respect for the military is as strong today as ever.'

'My older daughter married the captain of a nuclear sub in the North Sea Fleet, and her younger sister is dating the sub's political commissar. I whole-heartedly support their choices, since that means my family pretty much runs that boat!' He had a big laugh over that.

'My wife is the descendant of a White Russian family driven out of their country by the Bolsheviks. She's an ethnic Russian who was born and raised in China, and a citizen of the country. I was already wealthy in 1979, with thirty-eight thousand yuan in the bank. I've always been a risk-taker, but I never go into something without doing my homework. In the wake of the eleventh plenum of the Third Central Committee of the Chinese Communist Party, 1978 was a watershed year: rural reforms got underway, the communes were dissolved, contracts for tilling the land were issued. Well, the first thing that oc-curred to me was what the contracted peasants needed most were farm animals—horses and oxen. At the time, you could buy a good-sized horse in Inner Mongolia for four hundred yuan and sell it for a thousand anywhere south of the Great Wall. A two-year-old bullock bought for two hundred could be sold down south for at least six. I sold my profitable photography shop in the capital for ten thousand and used the money to buy thirty horses. Then I hired a herder to drive them south for me. But when they arrived in Hebei Province, both the herder and the horses were worn out from the trip and they couldn't find feed for the animals. I frowned at the sight, but then I had an idea. I drove the thirty horses into the Xuanhua County government compound. There, I looked up the county chief and told him I was a Mongolian horse herder who'd heard that peasants had been given contracts to till the land but that they were short of farm animals at harvest time. I said I'd brought thirty of my own horses down, fine animals I wanted to donate to the cause, free of charge. The official, whose name was Bai, rolled his eyes, but I assured him I wanted nothing for them. Well, when he went outside and saw all those fine animals, he said, "I can't accept those horses without paying for them. How's this, I'll give you eight hundred apiece." "Too much," I said. "Make it six hundred, and, if you need more, I'll go back to Inner Mongolia and bring you a hundred. You can send someone up with me, and I'll help with the purchases." So I became a horse trader that spring and turned a profit of thirty-eight thousand yuan. That county chief—he's now the deputy provincial governor—and I became fast friends.'

'With money in the bank, it was time for me to get married and start a family, so I decided to go back home and realize my youthful dream. I'll let you in on something: I've always been secretly in love with Lu Wenli. So I decided to buy her father's truck as a sort of gift, then drive it back to Inner Mongolia with her by my side to do something big and make a bundle. I asked around and learned that the state farm had been converted over to the contract system, and that Lu Tiangong was now the proud owner of that truck. So I sent a telegram offering him eight thousand, a high price by any standard, exactly what a brand-new Nanjing-built Great Leap NJ130—styled after the Gaz 51—went for. His old truck was worth two thousand, if that.'

'When I gave him the eight thousand yuan, I said it was a gift and that I had a hidden motive—like Xiangzhuang performing a sword dance to cover his attempt on Liu Bang's life. "He Zhiwu is buying your truck in exchange for the hand of your daughter," I told him. He laughed. "Don't think I didn't know that," he said. "You can't hide the bad water in your belly from me. But whom she marries is up to her, not her mother and not me. You're on your own. But, my young friend, I wouldn't count on it if I were you. The son of Deputy Party Secretary Wang has his eye on her. Between you and me, the shifty-eyed youngster looks like a bad piece of goods. But he *is* the son of a deputy Party secretary, and, if it's okay with Wenli, her mother and I will have to go along with it. No matter what happens after that, we'll have the honour of being related to the deputy Party secretary for as long as it lasts."'

He Zhiwu said he showed off by taking a few turns around the village in his 'new' Gaz 51. 'What can I say, I was young and stupid! I drove straight to the county capital. You're wondering when I learned to drive? In 1976, when I was working as a carrier in a brickyard, I struck up a friendship with a truck driver named Xu. He taught me. Back in the village, I'd been impressed by Lu Tiangong's driving skills. But I tell you, driving a truck is something you can learn in the time it takes to smoke a cigarette. So, anyway, I drove to the rubber processing plant to have a talk with Wenli. But the gateman said she'd been transferred to the post office in town. "How could the wife of the deputy Party secretary's son work in a rubber factory, where you can hardly breathe the air?" the old chatterbox said. From there I drove to the post office, parked the truck and bought a pair of new leather shoes at a department store down the street. They were so stiff I could barely walk, and it felt like everyone on the street was staring at my feet. As soon as I entered, I spotted Wenli—she was behind the stamp counter chatting with a middle-aged woman. I walked up and said, "Lu Wenli, I'm He Zhiwu, your primary school classmate. Your father sent me." She didn't know what to make of me for a moment, then she asked in icy tones, "What is it you want?" I

pointed to the truck parked outside. "That's your fa-
ther's truck," I told her. "He sent me to pick you up."
"I'm working," she replied. "That's okay," I told her,
"I'll wait in the truck till you get off."

'So I went back outside, climbed into the cab
and lit a cigarette. The city had absolutely no charm
back then. The three-storey county government office was the tallest building in town, and, as I sat in
the truck looking up at the red flag on the roof and
the pagoda pines behind the building, I was struck
by a particularly sombre emotion. I hadn't even finished the cigarette when Wenli came outside, so I
opened the door for her and she climbed in. I started
the truck up and drove off without asking a single
question. "Will you please tell me what's going on?"
she asked. I ignored her and sped down the road,
glancing at her out of the corner of my eye. She
started whistling, her arms wrapped around her
shoulders. That was new, and I liked it. The saying
that there's no telling what a girl will be like when
she grows up was right on the mark. After leaving
the town behind, I drove up to an empty field beside

the First High School playground and stopped. Why there? Because that was where she'd won the ping-pong tournament. I turned and looked at her. She really was a beauty, but she knew that something was up—she was immediately on her guard, not to mention a little peeved. "What exactly are you up to?" I could have beat around the bush, but I didn't. "Wenli," I said, 'I've liked you ever since we were in school together. And that day I rolled out of the classroom, I vowed to myself that, if I made it big one day, I'd come back and marry you. When you took first place over there"—I pointed to the high-school office, a one-time Christian church and the site of the ping-pong tournament—"I vowed to make something of myself before coming back to marry you." With a slight curl of her lip, she said, "And have you made it big? Made something of yourself?" "You could say that," I said. "How much do you make a month?" She wouldn't tell me. "That's all right, I already know. You make thirty yuan a month, three hundred sixty a year. Up in Inner Mongolia, I pocketed thirty-eight thousand yuan in the sale of farm animals—about what you could earn in a hundred years. I gave your father eight thousand for his beat-up old truck, so he and your mother would have all they'd need in their old age and you wouldn't have to worry about taking care of them. I have lots of friends up there and everything is all set. With that thirty-eight thousand as capital, in a few years I—no, we—can join the ranks of the hundred thousand crowd. Hell, we could be millionaires! You have my word that, one: you will never want for money, and two: I will always be good to you." '

' "Too bad, He Zhiwu," she said in that same icy tone, "I'm engaged to be married." "That's not the same as being married," I said. "And even if you were, you could get a divorce." "How can you talk like that?" she replied. "What makes you think you can come and mess up my life? The fact that you bought my father's beat-up truck? The fact that you have thirty-eight thousand yuan?" "Lu Wenli," I said, "I won't let you jump into a living hell because I love you. I've checked around. That Wang Jianjun is a no-good skirt chaser . . ." "He Zhiwu," she said, stopping me mid-sentence, "talk like that is despicable." "How can trying to save you be despicable?" I answered. 'Thank you very much," she said, "but you and I live in two different worlds, and I can take care of myself. You have no right to interfere." "Won't you even reconsider?" I asked. "Just stay away from me, He Zhiwu, all right? If Wang Jianjun knew what you were up to, he'd have someone beat you to within an inch of your life." I smiled. "I want him to know. Go tell him." She opened the door and got out of the cab. "He Zhiwu, don't lose sight of who you are over a little bit of money. Take it from me—money isn't everything." She turned and started walking to town. And as I stared at her back, I realized that she was right—that money isn't everything. But you can't do anything without it, that's for sure. "Take care of yourself, Lu Wenli," I thought.'

'I went home and knocked down a wall so I could drive Wenli's father's truck into the yard, where I covered it with a tarp and then repaired the wall. I told my father to look after it. "Look after it?"

he said angrily. "What's it going to do—sprout wings and fly away?" I told him to take the long view— that, one day, it would come in handy. After making sure my parents were well taken care of, I went back to Inner Mongolia with my brothers, started selling things like lumber, livestock and cashmere, and the money rolled in. I've got guts and I've got brains, and I'll tell you a little story to prove it.'

'In those days, the private sale of cashmere was illegal, which meant that smuggling a ton of the stuff into China proper could create huge profits— tens of thousands of yuan. Well, the government set up a checkpoint at the Wall, so I bought a pair of identical trucks, loaded one with cotton fabric and the other with cashmere. After covering the beds of both trucks with tarps, we drove them to a spot near the checkpoint, where we parked the truck with cashmere and drove the other one up for inspection. While the inspectors were checking the cargo, I plied them with cigarettes and a couple of bottles of good liquor and promised to bring them some things they wanted from down south the next time I came through. We crossed with no trouble. Then I turned around and drove back, telling the inspectors I'd left my spare tyre behind and needed to go back for it. I drove to where we'd parked the cashmere truck, and this time drove it to the pass and told them I'd found my spare. And they waved me through. Thanks to that little bit of deception, over the spring of one year, my brothers and I sold forty tons of cashmere and cleared four hundred thousand RMB. As the money grew, so did my stable of friends, and I was able to get residence permits for my brothers and find them positions in a local transport company. Back then, we had blind faith in residence permits and regular jobs.'

'I made another trip home in 1982 to build a new house for my parents. But didn't touch the old one where the truck was still parked. Just replaced the rotting tarp that covered it. My father was no longer on my case over it. "Zhiwu is a generous son," he said to my mother, "so there's no reason to question what he does." Lu Wenli had already married Wang Jianjun, but I hadn't given up hope. Then

I heard that life was treating her fine, and I figured it was time for me to get married.

'Word had barely gotten out that I was in the market for a bride when a dozen or more matchmakers showed up at our door. The girls they wanted to introduce me to would all have made good catches, but I said no to every one. Then a girl came to the house on her own. Who was she? Who else but my wife, Julia, who worked at the banner region livestock station. People called her "double death". From the rear, her mouth-watering figure was drop-dead gorgeous, but from the front her pockmarked face was death-dealing scary. "Elder Brother He," she said, "why do you want to get married?" I thought it over for a minute. "Two reasons: I want to have kids, and I need someone to cook and do the laundry for me." "Then I'm the one for you," she replied. I thought *that* over for a minute, then slapped my thigh and said, "You *are* the one! Let's go register right now." My marriage had tongues wagging all over the banner region. Just think—the richest man in the entire banner, He Zhiwu, chose a pockmarked woman for his wife. They didn't understand, of course—they couldn't. But you'll understand the minute you lay eyes on your two drop-dead gorgeous nieces and your soccer-star nephew. The only blemishes on my wife's well-formed face are the pockmarks, and those can't be passed on from one generation to the next. Her White Russian genes and perfect figure, on the other hand, can be, and were. Not only that—if I'd married a Han woman, we'd only have been allowed one child. But by marrying a White Russian, two were permitted by law, and it didn't take much to stretch that to three. So now you know how one of our nuclear subs was taken captive! Mixed-blood beauties are at the top of the heap—there's no comparison. I had it all figured out. If a man cannot marry the woman he loves, then he should marry whoever brings him the most benefits. For me that was Julia.'

'By the 1990s, I realized that the coastal areas beckoned if I was to really make a killing. So I looked you up to get help in transferring back to my home county, and from there to Qingdao. At first, my wife was reluctant to leave our home in Inner Mongolia but I told her I'd build a multistoreyed house in Qingdao'—he pointed to a large cream-coloured house—'that's it over there.' He then proceeded to tell me about all his great ventures, each of which I immediately forgot, since it was a succession of money spent, friends acquired, minor setbacks and huge easy gains.

'I wonder if you remember that skit we put on at the beginning of the Cultural Revolution?' I asked him, 'The one where I put on Teacher Zhang's tattered jacket and stuffed a basketball in front to play Soviet Russia's Khrushchev, and you combed white powder into your hair to play China's Khrushchev—Liu Shaoqi? Remember the lyrics? "Nikita is old, Shaoqi is young, on the stage together a duet is sung." Then I sang "Cook the potatoes and add some beef," and you sang, "Suffer minor setbacks, and enjoy huge easy gains." Well, that's the secret of your success—suffer minor setbacks, and enjoy huge easy gains.'

He thought about that for a minute, then said, 'In the main, yes, but not completely. A lot of the time I suffer huge setbacks without enjoying even small gains, easy or hard.'

'Are you referring to the purchase of Lu Wenli's father's Gaz 51?'

'That's pretty small-minded of you,' he complained. 'I never do anything without a cost analysis. My dealings with Lu Wenli were the only exception.'

'Did you go to see her after her husband died?'

'He was killed in an accident in 1993. By then I was in Qingdao, engaged in a steel business in partnership with the mistress of a certain big shot. Thanks to the big man's influence, we had a virtual monopoly in supplying steel for all of Qingdao's construction projects. I was enticed by the news that Wenli had been widowed, and I told your sister-in-law what had happened between us. With remarkable generosity, she told me to go get her and bring her home with me, either as a formal wife or as my mistress. But before I had a chance to go to her, she came to see me. Wearing a black skirt and white gloves, she was heavily made up and still beautiful, even as she approached middle age. "He Zhiwu," she said, dispensing with pleasantries, "I've managed to make it through the hard times." This was the time for me to be direct. "What is it you want," I asked her, "to be my wife or my mistress?" "Your wife, of course." "That won't be easy," I said. "The best bet is for you to be my mistress. I'll build you a house by the seashore and take care of all your expenses." With a mournful smile, she said, "Then I won't trouble you any longer." '

'Well, it didn't take long for news that she'd married Big Mouth Liu to reach me. So, taking two bottles of liquor and two cartons of cigarettes, I drove to the vacant lot in front of the Jiao River State Farm, where I revealed my admiration for Wenli to her father. I sat there, drinking and smoking and thinking. I'd always prided myself on my ability to read people, to know what was in a person's heart, when in fact I was judging people of virtue from the perspective of my own petty interests. The reason I'd been so successful figuring out what was in people's hearts was that most of the people I knew were as petty as me, whereas Lu Wenli was one of the righteous ones.'

The night before I left Qingdao, I had dinner with He Zhiwu at his house. His wife made seafood dumplings and, in true Gaomi fashion, prepared a bowl of garlic paste. An overweight, warmhearted woman, all it took was one look to know that she was a good wife and loving mother. We were well on our way to getting drunk when He Zhiwu turned off the light and told me to look at the kitchen window. Reflected on the glass was a series of bronze coin patterns, round, with square holes in the middle, sparkling like gold. I asked where the reflection came from, but he didn't know. 'I'd love to know,' he said, 'but all my attempts to locate the source have failed. None of the big houses by the sea have a hold over me. This is where I want to be.'

I nearly called him a miser, but held back. The more money people like him have, the greater their superstitions. Wanting to hear only fine-sounding talk, they scrupulously avoid inauspicious terms. So, instead of 'miser', I said 'a beneficiary of the god of wealth'. He liked the sound of that.

'Only a successful writer could come up with the perfect metaphor,' he said.

He Zhiwu phoned me after I returned to Beijing to tell me he'd found a piece of land by the ocean at Longkou, where he wanted to deal in real estate. 'Are you free to come see me?' he asked. 'The fellow who runs the land management office here is Zuo Lian, son of Chief Zuo, head of the Huang County Work Station, the fellow you worked for soon after you enlisted. Zuo Lian's face lit up when I mentioned your name. He said you'd watched him grow up.' I considered it for a moment, but in the end came up with an excuse not to go.

8

This May, Gaomi County Departments of Culture
and Radio and TV held the first ever *Maoqiang* per-
formance contest. Chief Lu of the Department of
Culture personally came to Beijing to ask me to serve
as judge. It would have been ungracious to refuse, so
I said I'd be happy to do it. Three years earlier,
Gaomi's *Maoqiang* had been designated as a living national cultural heritage. In order for this dramatic
genre to be passed on to future generations, the government and Party headquarters had decided to

establish a Youth *Maoqiang* Troupe, for which forty
primary-school children would be sent for training at
the Weifang Art Academy and be given career as-
signments upon graduation. Great importance had
been placed on this, thanks in part to the TV contest,
and there were more than five hundred applicants.
Every day, acquaintances, friends and relatives came
to the guesthouse to seek my help in getting their child
admitted to the troupe, and it rapidly started to annoy
me. I couldn't return to Beijing, since I was expected
to work with literary officials to spur the creation of
plays for the *Maoqiang* troupe, so Chief Lu found me
a room in another hotel to keep me from being
hounded. But, believe it or not, the very day I moved
in, I received a text message on my cell phone: 'Dear
old classmate, you probably don't remember me. I'm
Lu Wenli. I'm down at the hotel registration desk.
Would you mind coming downstairs to see me? I'll
only take five minutes of your time.'

We took a table in the hotel bar. When the
waiter came, I asked what she'd like to drink. 'Do
you serve alcohol?' I wasn't expecting that.

'Of course we do,' he said with a superior smile. 'What would you like?'

'I don't care, as long as it's alcoholic.'

The still smiling waiter looked at me.

'Two red wines', I said. He went down the list of choices. 'Just bring us the best.'

'The drinks are on me,' Lu Wenli said, 'I insist.'

'No need,' I said, 'I'll put it on my bill.'

She didn't react right away, but then said faintly, 'Oh, I forgot, you're a celebrity now, and I can't see you except on TV.'

'Now you're exaggerating,' I said. 'A con man fears nothing more than a fellow villager, except maybe an old schoolmate. But you and I were more than classmates—we shared a desk.'

'I didn't think you'd remember.'

'You're joking! After fifty, you can't remember what happened yesterday but the distant past gets clearer every year.'

'I know what you mean,' she said. 'Those days are starting to enter my dreams.'

'That just proves we're getting old.'

'A man's in his prime in his fifties,' she said, 'but at that age a woman's an old witch.' She was wearing a baggy black skirt, but not baggy enough to hide her thickened waist. The long, thin, delicate face I remembered was now moon-shaped and her lids drooped over eyes notable for their dark circles. When our wine arrived, we touched glasses and she took a big drink.

'How is Teacher Liu?' I asked.

'Gone,' she said with a sigh.

'How . . .' I was stunned. 'He was only in his sixties . . .'

'I'm afraid I'm like a black widow . . .'

'Please don't talk like that.'

She took another drink of wine as her eyes glistened with tears. 'Life has been hard on me,' she said, looking me straight in the eye. I'd have liked to make her feel better, but I didn't know how. So I just held out my glass to touch hers again. This time she tipped back her head and emptied her glass. 'But let's not talk about that. I have a favour to ask.' She took out a photograph and handed it to me. 'That's my daughter, Liu Huanhuan. I signed her up for the *Maoqiang* youth troupe exam. She's passed the first two stages and is now on the list of sixty. All the other families are working hard to get their children selected, I hear, so I swallowed my pride and here I am.' I studied the photograph. Liu Huanhuan, large mouth and eyes, thanks to Teacher Liu, but almost a spitting image of her mother. I vaguely recalled hearing the judges mention the name of Liu Huan-huan, so I sent Chief Lu a text message and got an immediate response: 'Supremely qualified, if only two were selected, she'd be one of them.' I showed the message to Lu Wenli, and the floodgates opened. 'You can breathe easy now, can't you?' I said.

'Thank you,' she sobbed, 'thank you so much.'

'Don't thank me,' I said. 'Your daughter's the one—qualifications, potential, exam, all excellent.'

'I know what's happened here today,' she said. 'Thank you, my old classmate.' She reached into her purse and took out an envelope. 'There's ten thousand in here. I hope it's enough for you to treat Chief Lu and the others to a bottle of something nice . . .'

I thought it over for a moment. 'All right, old classmate,' I said, 'I'll take it.'